Praise for *In the Year of Long Division*

"As it has been with every new writer of intricate beauty and substance, so it must be with Dawn Raffel, a writer who is, in Gerard Manley Hopkins's words, 'spare, original, strange.' Here again is the joy of wonderment, of first discovery—a book to ponder, to read and reread, to share with other lovers of literature, to give as a gift—which is what *In the Year of Long Division* was to me."
—Tillie Olsen

Praise for *Carrying the Body*

"Dawn Raffel is one of America's freshest voices since Faulkner. *Carrying the Body* isn't read. It's absorbed through the pores."
—Patricia Volk

"This taut, evocative tale of two sisters, a child, an insensate father and a dead mother, is a kind of family horror story in the manner of the grim talk of The Three Little Pigs, told and retold here."
—Robert Coover

"From the moment you begin reading, Raffel's writing snatches the breath out of your body and engages you in untangline the mystery of this family."
—Virginia Holman, *USA Today*

FURTHER ADVENTURES IN THE RESTLESS UNIVERSE

DZANC BOOKS

1334 Woodbourne Street
Westland, MI 48186
www.dzancbooks.org

These stories were first published in the following magazines. Grateful acknowledgment is made to their editors.

"Near Taurus" in *O, The Oprah Magazine,* "Her Purchase" in *Web Conjunctions,* "All Along the Silk Road" in *Fence,* "Our Heaven" in *The Mississippi Review,* "The Interruption" and "Love" in *The Rake,* "Sibling" in *Black Book,* "The Alternate Palace" in *Lost,* "North of the Middle" and "Steam" in *The Brooklyn Rail,* "The Woman in Charge of Sensation" (in slightly different form) and "Coeur" in *NOON,* "The Myth of Drowning" in *Guernica* and also as a short film by Steven Richter, "Mighty Breakers of the Sea" in *The St. Petersburg Review,* "Taken" in *Sleepingfish,* "The Air and Its Relatives" in *Unsaid,* "Cheaters" and "No Place on Earth" in *Opium,* "Flesh, Blood" in *Hunger Mountain,* "Seven Spells" in *Open City* "Beyond All Blessing and Song, Praise and Consolation" in *The Antioch Review.*

Published 2010 by Dzanc Books
Book design by Steven Seighman
Cover art by Sean Evers

06 07 08 09 10 11 5 4 3 2 1
First edition March 2010

ISBN-13: 978-0-9767177-9-9

Printed in the United States of America

FURTHER ADVENTURES
in the RESTLESS UNIVERSE

stories by DAWN RAFFEL

DZANC BOOKS

CONTENTS

In memory of my parents

And for Cherie

Visible light covers only about one octave,
speaking in musical terms.

—Max Born, *The Restless Universe*
Translated from the German, 1936

NEAR TAURUS

After the rains had come and gone, we went down by the reservoir. No one was watching, or so it looked to us.

The night was like to drown us.

Our voices were high—his, mine; soft, bright—and this was not the all of it (when is it ever?).

Damp in the palm, unauthorized, young: We would never be caught, let alone apprehended, one by the other.

"Orion, over there." He was misunderstood; that's what the boy told me. "Only the belt. The body won't show until winter," he said. "Arms and such."

Me, I could not find the belt, not to save my life, I said.

Flattened with want: "There is always another time," he said.

He died, that boy. Light years! And here I am: a mother, witness, a raiser of a boy.

I could tell you his name.

I could and would not.

"Here's where the world begins," he said. I see him now—unbroken still; our naked eyes turning to legends, the dirt beneath us parched.

HER PURCHASE

The woman is awake now. She opens her purse.

Toast, eggs.

The road over-easy, or easy enough. Fork. A knife. Elaina—her name, the fact of herself, is stuck in her with consciousness, a vengeance. Caffeine. "Warm you up?" the server says. The cream is artificial.

Elaina, like any good mother, is fully and dutifully absorbed in a spill. "After a certain age," she says.

"What age?" the child, who is all too abundantly clearly hers—her flesh and blood, etcetera—says. Licked cloth, a scabbed knee; a hair, black, genetically impertinent, a fait accompli: split-end in the eye.

"Jerome, look," Elaina says. "Sometimes a bird flies into the glass."

"What on earth?" Jerome says.

The server is waiting, obtrusively. A smear is on the window.

Aggressively ribby—the shirt Jerome wears. Wherever it came from, she did not buy it—a gift, perhaps, or hand-me-down. A shade of blue. So much he will own, will bear about his person, that she will not choose.

Jerome appears to be bigger to her than the last time she looked, as well as, quite possibly, thinner. He is opening sugar, ripping up packets and pouring the contents into his mouth.

"Stop it," she says. Her stimulant is dripping. The car is on asphalt, gathering heat. She knows she doesn't mean it. Let him, she thinks.

Money on the table, a mint in the hand. "You'll rot your teeth."

"What about the bird?" Jerome says.

"Completely exhausted," Elaina says. She is turning the wheel. The year is half over. Children in doorways, a bike in a yard—banana seat—rooms and rooms within each house. Somebody old is out on a lawn—a woman to judge by the shape of the body, but this is a guess. Elaina will not look like that! A wind is up. An orange ball has been abandoned in a driveway. Here is the world as driven past: a hospital, school.

"Will you stop asking questions?" Elaina says.

Jerome says, "What?"—which means, she thinks, "Now tell me something else."

"The bird," he says.

"Ah, yes," she says. He is kicking the dashboard, unsafely in the front. "I ought to know better," Elaina says.

Jerome is seven and a quarter or a third. Closer to a third. He is belted at least; at least there's that. Elaina does not look her age, not all of the time, or some of the time, she tells herself, as if, she tells herself, this were a comfort, this time.

A house they pass is gingerbread. Hansel and the other one: Eat you up! She taught him that.

Lilacs are blooming. Here it is—Gretel! Another of her stories: His father groomed lilacs, and hasn't he, Jerome, heard? She pinned them, or she thinks she did, coiled in her hair, a petal to a curl. She will have to cut her hair. Of course, there is also a tale about that. Rapunzel or Samson. Drive, she thinks.

A girl with a basket.

Nothing in the glove, a pill or three. Her child's breath: Baby. A scent she is fond of.

"Mom?" he says. "Mom?"

❋

It is somebody's birthday, the road sign says, revisably, in plastic.

"Where is the freeway?" Elaina says.

The sign is on wheels. It is raining, a bit. There is bile in her throat.

"Happy..." he says.

She swallows, again.

❋

"Get that up," Elaina says. Spilt grape on vinyl. "Money on trees." Last stop for miles and miles, forever. A Slurpee, no less.

She ought to teach manners, but who has time?

Tissue and napkins, so flimsy what she gives him—a kiss. Another kiss, pulled over to a shoulder.

She ought to enforce better hygiene, she thinks.

"Sorry," he says.

A ruffle of hair, and reacceleration.

Jerome is reading the names on signs. "Menomonee." She taught him that. "Oconomowoc." "Ray-seen," Elaina says. Midwesternized. Bastardized. Directions too, Jerome knows. "Over the river and through the woods..." She taught him that. "South to Chicago." "One, two, buckle my shoe..." she taught him that. "I know an old lady who swallowed a fly..."

Perhaps she'll stop.

Two in the morning or four or worse. It's a brilliant motel, though, at least on the outside.

Jerome is rightly sleeping. The room smells of breath, and of yesterday's throw-offs. Where is that shirt, Elaina thinks. And why can't she take charge of her possessions? She kisses him, her son, and walks away.

Back and forth and back and forth and back and back and back she goes, a sheet to the breast.

There's a flicker in the bathroom.

The past never changes materially—visit and visit, Elaina thinks. Her head is in the basin. The dead are still dead. She splashes the water onto her face; she towels—absorption.

Slippers, a headache, ever so slight. The cells that must wriggle and wriggle and wriggle inside her. "One, two..."

A seed, a wretched pellet.

She smells Jerome's skin as she lies down beside him, divided, awake, and wonders, will she miss him?

"What?" Jerome says.

They are in the museum regarding bones. Under a limb: Jerome says he's thirsty. So much in the world! ("The Great Lake— look! Look, the Windy City!") The body is always insisting on something. This, that; more, yes. Forever the expense of it!

Gum she has to quench his need, excuses, postponement. "See," she says, "the size of this." A knuckle. The room. The thrill of extinction.

"See how enormous," Elaina says. "Consider the enormity."

Jerome is not stupid, Elaina thinks.

✵

Elaina says, "Weather."

Toes to the counter. Chicken on a spit. The beef is "with awe juice," the server says.

"I am lonely," Jerome says.

Shake of the month. Precipitation in a tumbler.

"Wipe your mouth," Elaina says. "And how can you be lonely when I love you so much?"

"Mom," Jerome says—a word that means anything and everything and nothing, a holder of space, Elaina thinks, a consonant receptacle. "Who said I was scared?"

"Ala mode," the server says.

Jerome has dessert. He has crackers in wrappers after dessert.

The windshield is salted with droppings and grit.

"I am not afraid," Jerome says. Things are underfoot again, despite her imprecations—rigid, articulated figures with what would appear to be lethal capability. Blade upon glass. "Rain, rain, go away." Jerome, at least, is singing. The pterodactyl jacket: She gave him that, didn't she?

They're entering an artery, a heart of a city.

Elaina is singing along: "…away."

He is looking, she is thinking, at a woman getting drenched. "Why not go home?" Jerome says.

❋

"Don't touch," she says. She is teaching him something. Showing him something: a woman who lived.

He is bunching her dress. So chilly in the gallery! Pulling her handbag, he leaves an impression: Jelly on a palm.

"The artist is famous for painting," she says. "But see how he sculpted, molded out of metal." The dancers' arms are open, uncorrodable. The mutinous body is captured, whole.

"Careful," the guard says.

"Drafty in the dressing rooms," Elaina says, "a life of no comfort, no money, disease—and yet," she says, "the beauty."

Fingers to anatomy. A glare in the eye. You, you, you: The guard's eyes hold accusation, she thinks. "Miss," he says. "Missus."

Jerome is spinning, in a flighty pirouette.

"Watch he doesn't hurt himself."

"What do you say we dash?" she says.

❋

She is alert, alert, aroil in the night, and in the morning again, in fact, and still, and in need of a tonic or another cup of hot.

"Five, six, pick up sticks…" She taught him that. "Seven, eight…" She taught him that. "Little robin redbreast flew up to a wall…" "Five, six, seven, eight…" And why can't she concentrate?

Elaina tucks him in again.

So many things she cannot be shut of, or not so fast, at least not yet.

There once was a lady who swallowed a substance, or lived in a shoe, or did not know what to do.

She looks at him. "Perhaps," she says, believing he's sleeping, "the bird will do anything to get at something sweet."

❋

"Here is where you rest your chin. Hold still," she tells him. A long line of children synthetically dressed is stretched out behind them.

Science and industry. Science and technology. Hands-on, the flyer said, but everything is virtual, incorporeal, here. There is a fast game of ball in which there is no ball. No net in the court. No messy abandon.

Here is a landscape: a digital myth, or a world made of light.

You can channel the future, for a fee. A snap of your offspring years from now—inevitable jowl, grayer teeth, a mole. Reliable, certainly: the weight that comes of living, with margin for error, or possibly grief.

"See how Jerome will look as a man!" Elaina says, prodding. So long they have stood here!

"Mom, I don't want to." She feels the body stiffen, changeable as that.

"Now," she says, "or never."

"Please," she says.

Then, "As you wish. Maybe there's a gift shop."

❋

"What if they left it open?" he says.

Twin beds turned down, a drip in the tap. "Left what?" Elaina says. "What if who left what?"

"All of them," Jerome says. "They could open the windows all over the world."

He lies alongside her. "Happy," he says. So high the boy's voice! She narrows her eyes the better to see him—palpable body, the face as it is—and all she says is, "Wait." She says, "Wait."

ALL ALONG THE SILK ROAD

The kids were in the water. At least, she thought they were. Beneath the umbrella—a sturdy, unlovely, brick-and-black affair—the weather undid her. A gift, this. It was not of her choosing. Somebody—who?—with a practical inkling had given them this, a present for the marriage, dependably wrapped. Up it went. A shadow on the belly in the middle of the day. And in the hand, from a chest, ice.

She willed herself upright. "Do you, by any chance, see them?" she said, put a chip to the breast.

Soaked trunks, a flounce at a haunch, sweet navels of girls, a careless bravado in the curve of the back, strapped toe. The moment of near-recognition lost.

Her hair, in a headband, frizzed with heat.

"What did you say?" He was curling the page.

"Do you see them, I said. I don't see them, I said. Look. Just look. Please look. Do you think I should worry? Do you?" she said.

He looked at her—she felt he did—as if he were trying to reach a decision. In his hand the book went limp.

The lake appeared swollen.

Somebody called out the name of a fellow—a famous

explorer—and splashed, and jumped. A boy the size (more or less, give or take—roughly) of hers. Skinny in the wing bones, and nevertheless obstructing the view. His shoulders were burning, already beginning to pinken in the sun. He would blister for sure, need an unguent at night.

Two syllables—an offering. A ball in the air.

Heat shrilled the voice, or else the limits of breath, the lack of power in her.

I think your mother is calling.

Look! At play on the water, thwackers of plastic, diggers of holes—see here, a passage!—a castle in the silt, or an attempt at least—no fortress to speak of—lacking form, the overly wishful industry of children. "Look!" she said.

They looked at her avoidingly. The others—she saw them. A glare on the current, deviled eggs. Somebody's mother but hardly theirs.

Eyes in the back of the head—not her.

"In the water, they were. Just a minute ago."

He stood there and stood there.

"Both of them, the two of them, how could they?" she said. "But could they?" she said. She summoned their faces, receding from her. What were they wearing, either of them? A birthmark, moles.

The smell of them. (She loved the smell of them asleep.)

Now, what was the height of them, the weight of them—facts—which a person in authority would rightly request?

Her knowledge was approximate if not lackadaisical. She knew them—hers! her children—mainly only obliquely, it seemed, by unarticulated sense, or the objects they'd touched, too close for description.

"Polo!"

She flushed. She felt herself flushing, ever self-conscious.

"Weren't you watching at all?" he said.

❋

She was frightened of wind.

❋

This is what she watched at night, or rather, what she minded: the breathing—quick, too entirely quick—and flushing, the rising of the ribs. There was always a little light at a curtain, a street awake. She looked in rooms. She was frightened of heat when there was no breeze. The house seemed to vibrate, irregular, beating, a clock in the bedroom (master), built-in, ticking, slow: a lost minute in the day.

Things glowed at night. Appliances. So much she had been given (a shower for her!). And still in mint condition, sort of. The flame in the furnace was bluish in winter—she saw it, she did—in a child-sized window, an opening, a necessary menace, a toy. There was a voice she intended to find and disable. Press to quit. In the bosom, an almost mechanical compression. And in summer, a fan about to tumble, a bulb the wrong wattage, and close, too close, to a delicate shade.

❋

She was frightened of the current, afraid—yes, she was—of being carried away.

❋

"Yes, I was," she said. "I was. I was watching," she said, insisted to him. Because, of course, it was so. The house and its contents. The children. Herself. She was watching her husband sleeping, it seemed, or reading, it seemed, dogging a page, or walking away from her, it seemed—as he was, to the water, with nothing in his hands.

❈

This is not a true story. Nevertheless, she was frightened of cold, and had a tendency, at times, to overdress.

❈

She went walking alone along the lake, in the elements, wakeful, in the night, in rain. Night after night: a sweater, a jacket, forever a hood (unruly hair), against better judgment. She oughtn't to go about like that; he'd told her that. The danger! She walked to where the children had played, hands up the sleeves of the opposite arms, poked a toe to an already fallen structure, sunken in, to parts of things abandoned. A handle to something. Body of water; a woman washed to bones: There was a myth about this, if she could only remember. She had grown up far from here. She had lived on a river, the bed of a river, a gentle stream, and yet a child had died there. Blink of an eye. He was given to irritation, it seemed, this man she had married—a check out of order, a drawer stuck—and she to bouts of sentiment and also to rage. Tip of the tongue. "Your problem..." he suggested. She fought to retain things...a story, a list, or an important precaution. A wind rose at night. She had a boy and a girl, tucked in—tucked in and kissed—before she left them and thought of them and walked; she had a house full of foodstuffs and other provisions—yes, she did—and she was chilly or thirsty or hot or short of breath, and always, it seemed to her, late.

She had been raised to believe that any body of water was serious business—and also, the effects of the sun.

Insubstantial, she thought, the time that had elapsed, and this was what she'd told him.

She listened to voices. The children—the ones who were clearly, robustly, loudly not missing—weren't hers.

"No more than..." she'd told him. Inconsequential—that was the word she had meant to say.

There were—conceivably, in all probability—pills for her condition, whatever it was. There were sensible relations, as has been stated; pages of notes.

When she walked the riverbed, the width of the house, the battered path along the lake, she would cover her shoulders, or fingers, or mouth.

The town of her birth had been razed, or at the least, rearranged, made unfamiliar to her.

She could guess at an outcome.

Or cover her tracks.

She could skirt recrimination.

But that was back when nothing was at stake.

❋

The water had risen.

❋

A whistle blew.

A hole filled up.

Split second—the lifeguard, someone else's fracas: a blow to a bony, sunburned arm.

"Cheater!"

"I called it!"

As if out of nowhere, as if they had been there all along: They shrugged at her, reached hands beneath the chest's lid (such icy and relieving treats, under the umbrella). She saw that he saw, them, her husband did, from where he was standing, doused.

Look at them! A boy and a girl, beneath the shelter that had been so reliably purchased, pitched in sand.

She was frightened of watching.

OUR HEAVEN

"A fluke, an infection—in the lungs," our mother said.

"God," our mother said to us, standing by the telephone, confirming arrangements.

Roses in the garden, a finger in the dial. You could call out a window just as well. Where we lived were starter houses, latticed and treated, each house alike in dimension and plot.

The child who had died used to follow us home, a little brother we could already scarcely remember—neighbor's boy.

This was the way that we learned about heaven.

A woman in her sweater used to shiver on a porch. She was out in the evening, a house away from ours. Her boys were who-knew-where—in the bushes, perhaps, where we were known to play war. Or in the street, kicking cans, and, on occasion, each other, and us, too. They had soundalike names.

Germs, she saw. "Bacteria," she said to us. Duck, duck, goose and doctor with those downy boys of hers. Show and don't tell. Scraped, we knocked. She would give us a bandage for anything cut.

She had lost the children's father. "Marrow," said our mother.

We would lie on our backs and watch the birds race south. Maple and elm leaves: bags full, we saved—till we threw them away.

The gunner on the corner took to aiming her rifle.

"Dinnertime," our mother said. Her watch was in the shop again. "Crazy," she said.

And as for the shuddering mother, who had once been a nurse, "She wouldn't be so cold," our mother said, "if she would eat. Now eat."

※

My mother wants to tell me where the car is being serviced. "If something should occur," my mother says. She says it's at the Crystal-something and I ought to pay attention.

The telephone is beeping.

Someone has a mass, she says.

"The key to the house—"

Call-waiting turns out to be my long-distance carrier making an offer.

When I click back, my mother isn't there.

※

Up to the tower was 420 something steps, one of which was broken.

We could see us from there—our house, almost, or think we could, or someone's house, or fake it. We could squint there as if we could see ourselves playing, whacking a ball or skipping rope, unparticular children. Sometimes we could barely even tell ourselves apart.

Chicago was not visible.

The lake was an ocean—to us, it was.

※

"Guess where we're going?" our father said. "Cessna," he said. "A Piper Cub." He had been in the Air Corps during the war, of which we did not speak. A master of circuitry, he'd wanted to fly. The uniform hung in a bag in the cellar.

"Tell us," we said.

They had bitten him bloody, the insects had.

He had rigged what was airborne, readied it for discharge.

On display, the tea set from Japan—red cups.

A job in Chicago had fallen through. It was a problem of faith, our mother said. A trained engineer, he'd flipped a room of furniture (the family business, an issue of fallback) for hours of flight.

There was a medal on the premises.

Stuck in the plane, our faculties roiled. The royal us, sisters, doubled up in back. We vomited—takeoff. The whole world tilted, in a slant, through a windshield, beautiful—and down at last, reeking of puke.

Our mother was waiting on the ground for us.

We were taught to spray the telephone for reasons of hygiene.

Our grandparents drove up the block, and the world came to look. That car a boat, our mother said, after so many lifetimes of never enough.

Down on the corner, the gunner fired shots.

The bachelor uncle—our grandfather's brother—was in from Chicago. He sat in the back. Most of them had died by then, the siblings they'd had. TB and such. The complications of a bris, in one mortal instance. We did not observe. The uncle was rich from betting on something. He spoke about people we had never met—the kid who had crashed in the air, in France.

My sister and I piled in for the ride.

The brother of the child who had died had been haunting the bushes.

Horses and futures, bellies of pork. He lived alone, the uncle.

Into his nineties, our grandpa continued to drive that car. He would enter people's driveways, thinking they were streets to someplace else.

"Run past the corner as fast as you can!" The gunner was out, or so we had been told, and did not abide children. Dared, we gawked: the soundalike boys—whose mother occasionally raised her hooded head, the boy who'd lost his brother, the girl who in a few more years would be killed by a bomb that was meant for someone else.

The neighbor girls said, "Shut your eyes."

We peeped, of course. We scouted containers from in back of the drugstore. Redeemed illegally: a coin in the palm.

Our dad was working overtime. The miracle was Herculon, the fabric indestructible, and also—save your investment!—Scotch Gard; spray it and no stain was ever absorbed. The family store was decked out and festive: Orchids for ladies on Mother's Day, a dozen to a box, plus pins. We helped to hand them out. At Christmastime a glittered tree, not home, but here, as a business decision. Ashes in glass, the angel on the door.

They poured water on our heads so we wouldn't go to hell. It was sweet as a stolen candy in our mouths.

❋

When our father died, there was no one who knew where the car was parked.

The day the boys' mother, colder than ever, rang our bell to complain—Tim, Tom—we were listening in. It was true, what she said.

We were not to play doctor again, our mother said.

❋

Our father offered everyone who pulled up the dandelions a penny a pop. Our lawn sprouted children, some we did not know. Scattered by the fistful. Kicking up daisies. Our father in the doorway stood there and laughed.

The roses were in bloom.

He had his wallet in his hand, and the intent to make good.

The elm trees had their limbs sawed off.

A shot was heard.

Heads, stems: Everything uprooted on the lawn began to turn.

❋

My mother cannot climb so well, a problem with a tendon. She also, I can hear it on the phone, has a cough.

"Do you remember those boys who ran away?" she says. Our fellow transgressors. Stealers of things that were already empty. "Listen," she says. "They came back home. But maybe that was years ago." There is something she is taking to reduce the inflammation. "Didn't I tell you?" my mother says. "I want to say they're living somewhere else."

❋

We would fly on the lake—the brotherless boy often giving us chase—stunned with the pleasure and brought to our knees.

"Smell the flowers," said our mother.

He pummeled us, gently.

Our father would take us off to the air shows. See the pilots' figure-eights! Full-steam ahead, they had military know-how. Hop on a wing!

Our fingers were stained.

Precision was the issue.

When we wiped them down again, our skate blades gleamed.

❋

Our father would sometimes speak of the bris, a handed-down tale from before he was born, the infant too fragile. Not a slip of the knife, but a cold in the room, contagious. The boy, our father said, had no resistance in him.

"Religion," he said.

❋

There was a name in the sidewalk, written in cement.

❋

Our father one Sunday drove to Chicago.

The bachelor uncle had saved too much. Papers and papers: currency, insurance. News, old news. The records of the cousins who were killed back in Poland. "Mass grave," our father said, and never spoke of this again.

Down in the cellar, the bagged clothes stank. No one had touched them. "Except," our father said, "they were buried alive." Were they breathing in the earth? We went down to sniff.

Nights we had nightmares.

The uncle was interred, of course.

I have no idea where the papers have gone.

❋

My sister and I like to drive past the house whenever we're in town, which is rarely together. The elm trees have vanished.

The rifle on the corner, which should, by all rules of convention, have fired to a logical dramatic effect, to the best of our knowledge never did.

There is no one who knows us—what did we expect?

❋

My mother is telling me what's left, to be divided when she's gone. "Certificates," my mother says. "The medal, your father's—"

Someone is trying to break in on the call.

"Prayer book," my mother says. "You know that he kept it? The watch set with stones—are you with me?" she says. "Listen," she says, "with a little repair, it could still tell time."

THE INTERRUPTION

I heard a story at my great aunt's place, which I told to my sister long-distance on the phone. Well, first I said, "Did you know her real name?" because I knew or suspected that my sister did not. I will not repeat it here. But one of the cousins, a man whom I had never before had occasion to meet and whom I doubt I will meet again, explained over coffee, and after the whitefish salad was served, and after I took off my funeral heels, and while we sat watching the boats that were sailing along the lake, through the great, paned windows of my great aunt's apartment where she had passed so many years in bed alone—for the most part alone—how it was that our great aunt came to be born in Chicago.

"Our story begins in Poland," I said.

"Where?" my sister said.

"You heard me," I said. I was walking through my living room.

"Where? Where in Poland? Was it the city where the cousins were buried?"

"I didn't think to ask," I said. "It wasn't that side."

"I know but—"

"Sorry," I said.

"Is that your line?"

"They'll go away. So anyway, our great aunt X's mother was born in Poland, but fell in love with a man who was German. She followed him—"

"Uh, oh," my sister said.

"You know," I said. "But when she arrived, the lover deserted her. Very sorry story. And so, at least according to the cousin—"

"What cousin?"

"I told you," I said. "So rather than go back to Poland alone, she stayed as a tutor or governess—whatever they called it—"

"In Germany?" my sister said.

"I said that," I said. I put a book on the shelf. I was straightening up as I was speaking to my sister. "A friend of the family played the violin—a star of sorts. Anyway, he fell in love—"

"Aha," my sister said.

"Not yet," I said. "She didn't care. He played for her. He courted her. Nothing could move her."

"But," my sister said.

"Finally, the story goes, she agreed to marry him only on condition that he take her to America—Chicago, where her sister had settled."

"And?" my sister said.

"This was all before the war. Meanwhile, the cousin said—meanwhile, the lover who'd left her married someone else and had a family with her. Of course—you know. The lover, the children—none of them survived. And now that I think of it, the family in Poland...what?"

"Your phone."

"It will stop in a minute, I think," I said.

"That's horrible," my sister said.

"Listen, there ought to be a moral to the story, or anyway a point."

"Like what?" my sister said. "God has a plan? What kind of a—"

"God?"

"Plan," my sister said.

"Hang on," I said.

"But anyway, did that man—" my sister said.

"If you change your name," I said.

"Don't interrupt. The father. The husband. Aunt's X's father. Did he, when he came to Chicago, continue to play?"

"What?" I said.

"The instrument."

"Well," I said. "Great Aunt X could sing, I'm told. Although I never heard her. But what I was saying—"

"What are you saying?" my sister said.

"There is someone who apparently really needs to reach me." My sweater was itching.

"Wait," she said. "Just tell me this. Who do you think she loved in the end?"

"Who?" I said. "Great Aunt X? Or Great, Great—"

"The mother."

"I've really got to go," I said. "What are you asking? The one who broke her heart or the one who saved her life?"

"Which?" my sister said. "And how do you know that one of them didn't do both?"

"Or maybe her child."

"Or maybe her sister," my sister said.

My hand was on the button. "Forgive me," I said.

SIBLING

And so there were two of them, boys, snug in their little knit caps. One boy was sleeping. "Mama," said the other, the one who was riding upright, in front in the front-and-back stroller.

"See there," the mother said. "The moon, do you see it?"

"Undo me," the boy said. He tugged beneath his chin.

"Not yet," the mother said.

"Hold on," the mother said. "Your hat!"—for he'd flung it.

The stroller reversed. There issued sounds: a wheel against something, a stump or a root, the howl of a creature summoned, arisen—frantic for the breast.

THE ALTERNATE PALACE

The woman was screaming murder down the hall. I could hear her through the door. The man I was with lay in bed, tilted up. "Will you listen?" he said. I was wearing a mask.

I was married to him.

The linen was a mess.

It had been this way, like this, for days. There was a portal in his arm and a tube in his nose, and out the window lay the city, alive. We could see downtown, the river too. There was oxygen in there, in the tube. On TV there was a scandal. A colonel was speaking. "Ahem," the colonel said.

He had been coughing, my husband had, and losing weight. His lungs were filled with fluid. The fluid was red.

The colonel said "contra."

Data was taken, a quantity of blood.

"Consumption" was a word not said. Nevertheless, they were frightened, it seemed, the servers with the trays, and left them lying in the hall.

Underneath the mask, my face was hot. It was summer—the Fourth of July, in fact. I went out to get the tray.

The woman had thoroughly quieted herself when the doctor came to look, and so, the nurses said, he discredited reports. She waited until he was just beyond hearing. "Murder," she hollered. "Call the police!"

The dinner on the tray—there was cutlet, I think, and cubes of things—looked good to me.

There was a little chocolate cake with a toothpick flag. I was that hungry.

※

The woman with the basket of wash is me. I am a failure at folding. The bedding is crushed. The shirts are getting bigger: boys', men's.

I am sensitive to noise in this house of ours, where until rather recently we have not lived.

I have failed to even make an appropriate attempt.

※

The teacher was giving us a lesson in faith. She said, "Faith is a process," or something like that, to that effect. She gave us examples, and passages to read. I left the pages elsewhere, I believe.

※

At night, each night, I left the hospital for home. Where we lived, more or less, at that time, was a box. My husband was confined to isolation in the ward but the bathroom was shared with a patient who, going by the evidence, was stricken with a terrible and new disease. My husband had an old disease. "I think I am a danger to him," my husband said.

The woman was screaming as I walked down the hall

to where the elevator was. "Call 911!"

I rolled my sleeves.

The nurses went about their night and did what nurses do.

❋

I have often been accused of disregarding the subject. But while we're on the topic, they used bleach to clean up with after a procedure.

❋

The teacher was saying, "God's voice is on the waters." She told us, if we could, to dress in white.

❋

"Listen, I can listen to the hearings," he said. He was watching an investigation into weapons. I could hear it on the phone. I was sitting at work, eating fish from a container. At the time it was important—who said what and what we did. The woman sitting next to me was listening in. "Eee-rahn," she said. "Don't say 'I ran.'"

I went there with batteries and tissues and socks, and something to sip through a straw for myself, which I could do if I adjusted the mask, inadvisably.

"Opportunistic" the word we kept hearing. The cough had been suppressed by then.

The view overwhelmed me. Taxis and taxis; yellow, yellow everywhere, and gray, and rain; the tallest of structures—only one, on account of the angle, its double obscured. I had once had a drink at the top, on the deck, with a man who liked to talk about dreams. The man was from Chicago. He'd had the dream, he said, where he flew, and also the one we had shared about teeth.

My teeth were partly real.

The tube had been removed.

The man who had shared the toilet was missing, or so we had to guess.

❋

I was learning to use the computer at home. I was processing words. I kept violating something.

I was calling my husband at the hospital for help.

My doctor had told me I needed to be tested.

❋

I stood and watched the fireworks along with the others on top of the building. We saw them from the distance, miles to the east.

We couldn't hear a thing.

There were colorful fingers pointed at us, coming down from the sky.

I ate a carton of food with a wooden utensil, and dialed up the hospital.

"What was your fortune?" my husband said.

My dress was stained.

I said, "Wouldn't you like to hear what I saw?"

❋

My grandfather told me a story once, pertaining to a faraway country and king. My grandfather's friend had a valued position tidying the palace—the alternate palace, the residence for summer.

This friend let my grandfather enter in winter, and left him alone for a minute in the study. My grandfather sat at the desk of the king. He filched a pen. The pen had a feather and also a crest, my grandfather said. He had planned his escape. But the walls of the study, my grandfather said, were covered with various animal heads. Hunted down. The eyes, he said, were watching him.

He put back the pen.

The king was killed.

The friend was killed.

The people who lived in the village were killed.

My grandfather lived out his life in Chicago, selling cloth. His hands were red. Dry goods were his industry.

He sang with delight for us in another language.

"Listen," he said. "Vot I have is a story."

Still, I believe he wished he'd had the pen.

All of our sons have been named for someone else—in memory, or honor, or something akin.

I sat on the river, on the ferry one day, and watched the city burn. I was leaving, of course.

I am terrible at names and at faces—both. I cannot always recognize the people I know. But this I insist: I have never, I swear it, forgotten a voice.

After the food was consumed at night, I'd put the tray in the hall, and I would hear the woman raging.

Someone would come, sooner or later, my husband said, and take the remainders away.

LOVE

My grandfather wanted to tell me the story of the horse that died of heartache.

"What are you thinking?" my grandmother said.

The horse's name was Sully, my grandfather said. (Which must have meant something quite different in another language. I did not ask.)

"A beauty," he said.

He said it was true, the story he told: "Ven I vas a boy"—before the wars, before the influenza. He said Sully was owned by a neighbor he'd had. "A beautiful mare," he said to me. "Magnificent. The apple of the village. The neighbor vas poor, of course." At last and in time and at very great length, he was persuaded, this neighbor, with a marvelous regret, my grandfather said, to part with her, to sell her to a traveling show.

He missed this horse.

One day in the spring of the following year, the traveling show traveled back to the village. Everyone went, my grandfather said. Every last soul who could scrape the amount to pay for a ticket. "And vot do you think?" He raised his hands, reddened from labor. "Sully broke rank the minute she saw her old master again. A plume, she had. A feather. She ran to him, ran out of the ring." He saw through the fence posts, my grandfather did. "He threw his arms around her neck! But he could not afford to buy her back."

"And?" I said, though I had heard it before, and more than once, and asked again.

"The horse collapsed that very night."

He was old, my grandfather. "A plume this high."

"Why are you telling a story like this to a child?" said my grandmother, when all was done, as was her way.

She served us cake, golden.

I had a new question.

My grandfather chewed. "Vell," he said. There was no one alive in the village, he said, not anymore, at least not that he knew. The man did not get out, he said. "So far as I know."

"You know, there are people," my grandmother said, as she captured a crumb, "who eat to live."

"Ve live to eat," he said.

She gave him a napkin.

He died when he was very old. He'd stopped speaking English.

"What is this?" the night nurse said. "This language of his?"

NORTH OF THE MIDDLE

They are both of them, mother and daughter, inflamed by something minuscule, sneezing in tissues, covert sleeves, a hand.

The mother says, "Bless."

The daughter says, "God."

The mother says, "Look." She says, "Look at yourself."

The daughter is young. She is darling to look at, the mother says. "If only," the mother says.

"Stop it," the daughter says, the timbre dropped, as if some sort of gauntlet. "Mother," she says.

"All I am saying," the mother says.

The windows in this hotel will not budge. The daughter thinks mites must live in the air, or maybe the carpet, or else in the bedding—dust or other allergens. "Please," she says. "Pass me…"

The mother gives the daughter the thing that she asks for. "Whose idea, anyway," the daughter says, "is this?"

Neither she nor the mother lives in this country. "Neither here nor there," was how the mother had put it. "We'll meet in the middle, north of the middle."

"Here is a thought," the mother says.

"Just a thought," the mother says. "Listen to me, we could both use some color."

The daughter has something crumpled in her hand. She says, "Where?" She says, "Where is the trash?"

❉

The store smells of lotion, the daughter thinks, or of salve, or of sugar, or something artificial.

The mother says, "There."

The signs are in English.

In between floors, riding a step, they are poorly reflected. "I can't see," the daughter says, "enough to tell, to really tell."

"Let's just look," the mother says.

"Look at this," the mother says. She is judging a garment, holding it up.

"For me or for you?"

"You," the mother says.

"Me," the daughter says, "I am hungry, is what."

"Here is the mirror," the mother says.

The mother looks tired, the daughter thinks. The lipstick the woman, the certified expert, applied to her lips is bleeding into lines about her mouth.

The girl is smudged beneath the eyes from what the woman wanded in.

The mother takes tissue to work on the daughter, licking it.

"This is not us," the girl says.

❉

The mother and the daughter are sitting at a table. "Watch the rotation," the mother says.

The scene beneath them seems to turn.

"Careful," the maitre d' had said. "Watch your step."

The daughter sips.

"When I am married," the mother says.

"I said, when I am married," the mother says.

"All right," the daughter says. "We had this discussion, didn't we?" She is viewing her choices, sniffing in a napkin. "What is a tourtiere?" she says.

"After the wedding," the mother says.

"Yes," the daughter says. "I said alright."

"What was the question?" the mother says.

The daughter feels bad that the napkin is cloth. She should use something else.

"My new home," the mother says. "A week, then? A weekend? You'll come for a weekend."

"Didn't I say it?" the daughter says.

"Maybe a long one."

Here is the server. The dish, he says, is national and comes recommended.

The daughter assents.

"You will, then?" the mother says.

"What are you getting?" the daughter says.

The order is given. "I worry—you know that I do," the mother says.

"Enough," the daughter says.

"It's just—" the mother says. She is looking in her purse. She is fishing for something, the daughter thinks.

"Look at that," the daughter says. Something is blinking at the edge of their view. They are turning from it.

"There is never enough time," the mother says.

❋

In the night the daughter listens—she sits up and listens—as the mother sleeps.

※

The blush they have purchased, the daughter says, or rather, the mother has purchased for her, suits her a little.

"It does," the mother says.

The drapes are shut, the beds undone.

The daughter is standing inspecting her face, which looks, she thinks, like her mother's in features, if not in expression.

"Do you mind?" the daughter says.

"You're hovering," the daughter says.

"Not hovering," the mother says. "It's just you're not used to living with someone." She opens the drapes. She pulls at the windows, having forgotten, the daughter thinks, or else unwilling to remember.

"Glued," the daughter says.

"Gusendheit," the mother says. "What do you want to do today?"

"Don't know," the daughter says.

"God bless, I said," the mother says. She pulls out a guidebook. "Churches, museums...listen," she says, but the daughter is not listening. She scrunches her cuffs. The daughter has a scar, very slight, at the wrist from where the mother, the mother insisted, saved the daughter's life, or maybe only a limb. "You were walking in traffic," the mother had said. The nail left the mark.

"Getting late..." the mother says.

The daughter sees the mother is beautiful in profile.

"What did I say?" the mother says.

"There is plenty of time," the daughter says.

"It is only the season," the chemist says. Nevertheless, she has something to sell them. "Take it with plenty of fluid," she says.

"Try this on," the mother says. "I want to buy you something."

"Not my style," the daughter says.

"It could be," the mother says.

"I said, not my style."

"What is, then?" the mother says.

"Don't, now," the daughter says.

"Then talk to me," the mother says.

"I am," the daughter says. "I said I would."

The mother says, "Then, do you promise? Seriously, I am buying you this."

The daughter is eager to take her dose. "Water," she says. "You know I won't wear it." Later, the daughter will wish she had said something kinder or better, or, at the least, different. Already, she does. "Mom," she says. She touches the mother on the arm, on bone.

The daughter is holding a bag in her hand.

"When you come," the mother says. She is wearing a faint shade of blue on her lids, which are only the slightest bit swollen today. The concourse is crowded with what, to the daughter, appears to be families, and also with lovers.

The daughter is thinking of killing an hour, all the ways. Announcements are spoken. The floor is clean. The mother's plane is boarding first. Arms, scent, breast, breath— the mother surrounds her.

"Mother, please," the daughter says.

The mother is feeling for tissue again, the daughter thinks, inside her purse. But no, it is money.

"I don't need—" the daughter says.

The mother says, "Take it."

The mother says, "Call."

The daughter is jamming a bill in her pocket.

"Such a lovely getaway," the mother says—and then, as the daughter watches, is gone.

THE WOMAN IN CHARGE OF SENSATION

First, she broke her anklebone. How this was accomplished, I am not equipped to say. Will you listen to me? She could not abide a bath—no oil or Epsom—even when she could get wet. And now, you know, they had to keep her stable, immobilize the bone with a variety of substances, all of which were soluble, and therefore to wash it—the ankle, the foot, and, to get down to logistics, the neck—was rather out of the question.

"Can't," she said.

"Cannot," she said.

"Can't you please see that I'm sleeping?" she said.

She was knitting a scarf in a brilliant red.

She asked me just to use the cloth in places in between again.

She used the word *pearl*.

The bruises were looked at professionally. This was not a fall, they said—not simply a fall, they said—but likely a condition. They were firm about this, and spoke as if in confidence, if not out of earshot.

"Can't you turn it down?" she said. Voices, a faucet. "The phone off the hook," she said. "Just pay attention."

On the floor the atomizer lay where she had dropped

it, beading the plank.

"Careful where you step," she said. The room smelled expensive.

She gathered up pillows, in a strategy, apparently, to elevate herself—at least some of herself. She was ripping out something. "Look at," she said. Things wadded inside her. Additional symptoms: nostril, the works. She needed to flatten herself and pinch.

Balls of wool were on the throw. "It's crooked," she said. There was more of her broken.

The experts were summoned, consulted, apprised. These were uninflicted damages. Everyone was compensated.

There amid the draped sheets; a slung arm, this, that— "I'd call it disagreeable," she said in concurrence. She tapped on the drip. "Prop me," she said. "Lift me a little. Pummel and plump," she said. "Go ahead and hit."

She had what she'd made, retrieved from the house. It was as she'd requested. Needles too.

They told her to make a fist and squeeze.

"What was the question?"—the woman in charge of sensation, a nurse. Marrow, cells, etcetera. A density ratio. "It works like this."

It was a button and such. "Easy," they said. "Easy does it with that."

I was not next of kin. There was no one who heard me. They covered her later.

Salt was on her lip in there, and fluid leaking out of her. The odds were against this.

It was I who dried her. I wrapped the thing around my neck—tassels dampened—as she'd intended, arguably. I said the odds were against it.

The ankle was healing still, they said.

THE MYTH OF DROWNING

"Are you sleeping?" he said.

"Are you?" she said.

"I guess," he said. "What are you thinking?"

"Nothing," she said.

"Or nothing you want to say," he said.

"I didn't say—"

"Listen—"

"Goodnight," she said.

"Wait," he said. "Don't go to sleep angry."

"Who's angry?"

"Or cross," he said.

"Not cross," she said.

"What now?" he said. "What on earth is wrong now?"

"Nothing."

"Nothing. You know what I think?"

"No, what do you think?"

"Forget it," he said.

"No, tell me," she said.

"Please," she said.

"I'm thinking. That story you told…"

"Which?" she said. "What's that?"

"The wind," he said.

"I know," she said.

"The woman?"

"What woman?"

"The lake," he said. "The woman on the lake."

"The river?"

"The river. I guess it was the river. The woman who drowned."

"I'm beat," she said.

"Who was she?"

"No one."

"Everyone is someone."

"Okay, someone. But no one we knew. A story my mother told," she said.

"You sure?" he said.

"I'm sure," she said. "I think so."

"Oh," he said. "Still—"

"What made you think of that?" she said.

"Just..." he said.

"Shhh," she said.

"What is it?"

"The children?"

"The children are sleeping."

"But—" she said.

"Don't change the subject."

"It's late," she said.

"This house," she said. "It moves in the night."

"You mean it creaks," he said.

"It spooks me."

"Nothing but the wind. The woman," he said.

"What of her?" she said.

"How was it that she drowned?"

"Who knows," she said. "She couldn't swim. Or cramps. Maybe undertow. The undertow was wicked."

"You know what I mean."

"No, what do you mean?"

"I mean people were there," he said. "That's how you told it. A crowd on the shore."

"That's what the myth is: Drowning is noisy. It isn't," she said.

"It isn't," she said.

"I heard you the first time."

"Tired, I said."

"Broad daylight," he said.

"And shallow," he said. "No one could see her?"

"No one could see her distress," she said. "They looked too late. Or else they didn't look."

"I love you," he said.

"Okay," she said.

"What?" he said.

"Okay," she said.

"Me too," she said.

"Goodnight," she said. "Listen, I'm sleeping."

"You are?" he said.

"I am," she said. "I told you I was."

COEUR

"Look into the pumpkin's face," he says. Wiping the pulp off, side of a leg, he needs her to pay attention, he says.

"Mind yourself"—her mother's voice inside of her, serrated and worn. She should clean up the mess.

"Madre," he says. "Mama mia. Maman!"

The eye he has cut is a heart, she sees, if a heart were heart-shaped. "How do you say it in French?" he says.

She fires the oven.

"Salt," she says.

"You aren't even listening. Mother," he says.

"Buddy," she says, either scolding or pleading: Can't keep her hands off, not for long, and never could. "Hands to yourself"—it is the story of her life.

Once upon a time, there was a girl with an empty place in her glove, an actual person known to Faye or, at least, described to her, minus the details. There but for the grace of God.

A slip of the knife has ruined the mouth.

All of the faces she has known, has loved, has watched fall!

All along the walls, there are the marks of the boy, in pencil and in fingerprint. In crayon and craypa , wax, sweat, on paper and not, in pulp, in ink, in shadow, scratched.

The oven clicks.

She is squatting to his level. "Here is the way that you say it," she says.

❈

"Hold still," she says. "Don't move." She is tying a knot, or trying to. He holds a sword.

"Dagger," he tells her, by way of correction. Rubberized and bendable.

"I cannot allow," she says.

"I simply forbid," she says.

"You cannot walk alone," she says. "The river, and who-knows-who about. You know what could happen."

"How do you know?"

"Not going to say it again," she says. There is a hand in her pocket searching for something, a residue she feels against her teeth. "Not going to say it. Unpleasant," she says.

He is pulling the costume off himself, up over his head, the ends undone. Up, up in arms. Silvered legs are on the floor. She picks up the garment. The weapon has fallen. "Buddy," she says.

"Don't call me that."

"Señor," she says. "Monsieur?"

❈

"Hello?" she says. "I'm hanging up."

❈

She is holding a jacket, an empty sleeve. "I could tell you a story," she says, and does not. She is the keeper of mishaps: flukish and apocryphal, occasionally true. She holds it close: the story in the news about the woman who drowned. She'd been a woman who stole things, reckless and possibly somewhat distractible or, Faye thought, aloof. She had a beautiful name. She had a lopsided sidestroke, a light plait of hair. She had appeared, Faye thought, to be engaged, in a hurry, as Faye is herself, as if to finish up or polish something off.

❋

She says, "I haven't got all night."

She says, "Speed it along."

She says, "Here is a flashlight. Other hand."

She says, "At least." She is always, she is thinking, doing most of the talking.

"What at least?"

"At least," she says. She rights a strap. "At least it's not raining. Not too cold. Look," she says, for here they are, walking, persuaded into costume—the boy is, at least—and out of the house. "Ghost," she says, "Look, look, a little goblin! Lower the beam."

He does as he's told, illuminates a foot, the curb, a leafy menace.

The child of the woman who drowned is in the walkway, surrounded by men. She is smaller than Buddy, golden-haired. She is wearing a tiara.

Buddy says no. "Halo," he says.

❋

"Where is a match?" Faye says to him or else herself. "At least it's nice and warm in here." Disorder of the day: the newspaper spoiled with vegetable matter, marker, salt.

"Why did we walk away?" he says.

"Look up there"—there is a shelf full of things that are presumably dangerous and easy to reach.

She has the phone off the cradle.

"Mom," he says.

"Who is there?"

"Why?" he says.

She says, "I won't repeat myself," into the receiver. "Tell me what you want," she says. "This must cease. Buddy," she says, "please give me that."

"Why not just hang up," he says.

"I am," she says.

Flint. He is lighting the candle inside of the pumpkin, precariously balanced. Flesh is burnt inside the thing.

Faye has heard the breathing. She opens her mouth to feed herself handfuls. "Want some?" she says.

"You need to drip the wax," she says.

"Careful," she says.

"Let me," she says, and knows he won't.

"Seeds?" she says.

"I thought you were hanging up," he says.

"I did," she says, depressing a button. "Buddy, listen, at least you have me."

❋

"Curr?" he says.

"Coeur," she says. "The way that you say it," tucking him in. She knows it won't last. He'll be up in a minute. "A cur is a dog."

"It is?" he says.

"Yes," she says. "A mean one at that."

※

He proves her right.

"Can't sleep," he says.

"I know," she says. "Your father also never slept."

"My dad?" he says.

She ought to do something maternal, she knows. Tell him a story. "My mother would tell me a story," she says. "I just can't think."

"You said my dad."

"I did," she says.

"Tell me something else," he says.

"Like what?" she says.

"Something."

※

There's a crack in the glass in the morning; Faye sees it. "Look at the window," she says. "It's shot."

"Shot?" he says.

"Cracked," she says.

"How did it happen? Was it a bad guy?"

"No," she says. "I doubt it."

"I'll cut him," he says.

"It wasn't a bad guy."

"Who?" he says, "Who did it, then?"

"For certain," she says, "it was only the weather, or maybe a prank, or else the pane was unstable."

"Or maybe," the boy says, "it might have been a cur."

✷

The boy knows better. Of course he does. He will not rest. "Maman," he says. "You promised a story."

"Tomorrow," she says.

He says, "You said that yesterday. A promise is a promise. You said it yourself."

"You're right," she says. And she will not tell the boy about promises broken, the hair of the ghost. "Once upon a time," she says. "There once was a mother who loved her little boy…"

"Mom," he says. "A story. A real one."

"Stop it," he says.

"Get off me," he says.

"I can't," she says.

"Mom!"

"On the night you were born, there was a fire in the hospital."

"Really?" he says.

"Really," she says.

"Cool," he says.

"They sounded the alarm. Everyone evacuated, even the babies."

"Me?" he says.

"You," she says. "At least it was nice out." His father was there. It was he who'd cut the cord, had held the bloody scissors. "I thought it was a sign," she says.

"Of what?" he says.

"I really couldn't tell you."

"What happened?" he says.

"The fire," he says.

It had to mean something, is what she had thought. "What else?" she says. "They put it out."

STEAM

My mother called to tell me that today was her birthday.

"I didn't think," I said, "that you would be alive."

She wasn't, of course. In the morning I went to the pool where I go when I go to swim laps. The pool is high up and has a view of the city. After I swam, I went to see a movie. I could not go to work because a steam pipe had broken— exploded—outside the building, the high rise, that has my office in it. A violent plume had obstructed the sky, ruddy and thick, and there were shards flying everywhere, of masonry and glass. People were screaming, believing the worst.

I wished just a little that I had been there.

It was all of it cordoned: papers, files, information irretrievable, the windows blown. The news showed the street, laid bare save for rubble.

Outside the theatre, the rain fell hard. The roof had a leak. Drops, great drops, then showers of water poured onto the plastic— hefty, black—that someone had laid on the topmost seats. I had just come from a country, from visiting a country, where things like this happened. Water that fell rolled all down the floor. The handful of people watching the movie in the middle of the day in a city where things such as this were not prone to happen did not appear troubled. They moved to dry chairs. The star of the movie, a world-famous actress was dying and dying, and then she died.

I went home and baked treats to mail off to my sons via overnight service, throwing away all the ones I had burnt. There were many I had burnt.

I called my office voice mail.

My sister was not home. I left her a message, which might or might not have recorded, I thought.

My mother had called me the night before the morning she did not wake up. She was coming to see me, had purchased a ticket, would be here, she said. She said, "I have to get away." She said, "Out of this place." She wanted to talk about food we would eat, in the future, in the city. Bread from the bakery, Chinese, cake. She said, "I must." ("Must you go?" my great aunt said before she died.) My mother, I thought, did not sound distraught. But I have not told the truth. I didn't, in fact, speak to my mother on the night before the morning she did not wake up. I am off by a day, a week at most.

The call came at work. I was not at my desk. This did not matter. I said they were wrong. My stepfather lay dying himself on his side of the bed, and he was quite hard of hearing. The housekeeper found her.

The telephone, the catering, the burial, bills. The carpeting, the realtor asserted, had to go. It was I who placed the papers and tissues into the bag—it was a big, dark bag—and then I wiped the surfaces. The carpet was cream. It was all done correctly.

The corporate hotline did not have an update.

The boys sent a message from somebody's gadget in digits and type.

I cleaned up the kitchen. The call was my sister. I said, "What's new?"

"It's raining," she said.

"Here, too," I said, "and I am so far away."

MIGHTY BREAKERS OF THE SEA

All along the waterfront, the girls fan out. Look at them there! In red and in blue, in yellow, white. They are young, these girls; they are dressed in swaths of gauze. They are walking in the water.

The moment should be frozen. The story we are witnessing should have had a different start, such as, Once upon a time, or, In another country.

The water rises. The girls are subsumed—to the breast, the neck.

It is a very old tale.

The girl in yellow appears to be looking for something under the surface she will not find, or must not find. The other girls take her and lead her ashore.

※

"If," says the king of the kingdom to girl in the yellow. "If you find the feather, you may marry the prince." He says, "The feather is enchanted and will carry good fortune." The boy will be king regardless of outcome. The mothers are absent, as it must happen. The feather, according to the king, will be in water. "Come," the king says to the girl in yellow. "Do you not wish to be the wife and then the mother of a prince and then a king?"

He had buried his previous wife alive in ice, the prince had, for a minor infraction—a wayward glance, not even a kiss. The wife before that, a child, no less, not much past twelve, was believed to have been poisoned with a drop on the tongue.

The king takes the girl in yellow by the shoulder. Old as he is, he has all of his teeth. "Will you not look for the feather?" he says.

"But where?" she says.

"In the morning," he says, and shuts the girl in yellow in a room in which the window is broken.

Daybreak, a bird flies in through the frame. "I will help," the bird says. "If you will give me your pledge."

"What pledge?" says the girl. "And what if I don't?"

"Then you'll die," the bird says.

And so the girl clambers out through the window and follows the bird, at least as well as she can, because the bird is swift. "What have I promised?" the girl asks the bird.

"To keep me," the bird says.

The bird leads the girl to a very deep forest. "Bird, I am hungry and thirsty," she says.

They fly and they walk to a well that is deep. The girl looks down from the light into water. "There is no feather here," the girl says.

The bird is on the ledge.

"You misled me," the girls says, and drinks her fill.

Back in the palace, the king takes the girl in yellow, increasingly shabby, deeply to task. "No supper for you," the king decrees. "And as for the feather, if you don't find it , I will stone you to death."

The son of the king is playing a flute. The girl in red is dancing for him, ashimmer in jewels.

The king says, "The feather."

Daybreak, the bird reappears at the foot of the bed to the girl in yellow. "Do not fear," the bird says. "Follow me," the bird says.

"Why should I?" the girl says. "You failed me the last time."

"Because," the bird says, "you promised to keep me."

The girl appears not to believe she has made such a vow but follows the bird through the forest, and then to the field. Thorns pierce her feet, and her garment of yellow is stained and torn. "I am hungry and thirsty and dirty," she says.

Rain falls in torrents. "There," the bird says.

"Where?" the girl says. "There is no feather in the rain in the field."

The bird is in the grass.

"Then you are not looking," the bird says.

The girl drinks handsful and washes herself.

Meanwhile, the girl in white has gone to the sea in search of the feather alone, she has. "If I find the feather," she thinks to herself, "then the son of the king must marry me." The girl in the white trips on a rock, which is sharp, which is hidden by the water, which has risen to her eyes. There is nobody there. She drowns.

Back at the palace, the king shakes the girl in yellow until she cries, "Mercy."

"No supper for you," the king says.

Music is playing.

"One last chance," the king says. "If you do not find the feather—"

"I know," she says.

"Only the feather will save you," he says. "Do you not wish to be the wife and then the mother of a prince and then a king?"

"I wish," she says.

Meanwhile, the girl in blue, embroidered and sashed, is weeping by the sea, for she loves the king's son, and will never so much as glance at another.

Daybreak, the bird comes back to the foot of the bed of the girl in yellow, in the room where the table and chair are now broken. "Come," the bird says.

"Not the sea, and not the well, and not the rain," the girl says.

"Not the sea, and not the well, and not the rain," the bird says. "Nevertheless, you have given your promise."

Her hair hangs in clumps. From far down the hall, she can hear the flute playing.

"Follow me," the bird says, and so the girl follows—all through the day and into the next and into the next, her feet now bare. When she can't see, she follows by sound. When the wind blows, she follows by feel.

"Bird, I am dying," the girl says, as day finds the world again. The kings' men will hunt her.

Hungry and dizzy and thirsty and ragged, the girl in yellow spies a glass palace ahead in the distance, which, the bird says, is of another kingdom. Hour upon hour they walk and they fly. It disappears. "There is no palace," the girl says. "It was only a terrible trick of the eye. All you have done is swindle me."

"Then kill me," the bird says.

"Maybe I will."

"Go ahead," the bird says.

The girl grabs the bird by the neck and wrings. It dies in dirt.

"What have I done?" the girl cries and cries. "Now all is lost." And then the girl sees it: the feather in the broken body in tears. The feather is golden. She sits there awhile, in her dress that is yellow, aslump in the dirt.

She eats the bird. She sings in light.

The girl in yellow, bearing the feather, returns to the king. "Too late," the king says. "The prince has already chosen another." He turns the girl out.

The girl lays the feather under her pillow. She lives in a shack.

The girl in red is beheaded in the spring.

The prince becomes king. The streets are all paved.

Many years later, the prince who is king is disemboweled by his son. Asleep in a shack, a tiny old woman lies dreaming of flight.

All along the waterfront the girl in blue, who is ancient by now, who is shrouded by now, walks the skin from her feet until the blood leaves marks, until the bones leave tracks, until the wind and the water wash them away.

TAKEN

"Come with me down to the river," she said.

"Now?" he said.

"Now," she said.

"But it's the middle of the night."

It was the middle of the night. Their children were sleeping, and thus it was reckless. Nevertheless, they walked down to the water and killed the light they'd carried there.

The river was filled with what rivers are filled with.

"Listen," she said.

He caught his step. "What is that?"

"The current," she said.

"No, that," he said. "The planet."

"What planet? Oh," she said. "Venus?"

"It's early for Venus."

She threw in a stone. "I suppose," the woman said.

"Well, anyway," the woman said.

"Well, maybe," the man said. "Tell me what you think."

"I guess we ought to go," she said.

"It's something, I think."

The water was active.

Together they sat skipping stones in the dark.

THE AIR AND ITS RELATIVES

We cannot find the car in the lot, again. Our ears burn, or mine do. Wind off the lake holds a violence in winter. My father says nothing. The building from which we have just made an exit is already locked; its churning stars extinguished, planets suspended, moons switched off. It is a very old facility. It rests on a spit, a peninsula, a man-made extension, apart from the city, the center of the city with its steam and vibration. The lot is near empty, the sky too low. "Now I remember," my father says. "We're not here."

"Left," he says. "Go left at the light."

"I am trying," I say. I have failed the test twice: rolled over the curb, did not see the object. Nevertheless, I do as instructed.

My father is wearing a jacket older than I am, gotten in war.

There is a star on the windshield.

The car had resurfaced outside of the aquarium a half-mile inland.

"Stop at the stop sign."

"Which?" I say.

Cracked glass. Droplets.

"Hit the de-fogger," my father says.

"I know," I say. I do, in fact.

My father is pushing a button on the dashboard. Bone and vein and knuckle; the nails are not clipped. There is a scar on the hand.

There is a sigh of activation and the world becomes visible.

"Better," he says. "You're learning, I think."

Now we are only maybe ninety miles more from home.

❋

"Congenital," my father said, the time that he said it, describing the defect. Degenerative, and worsened by the decibel. The permanent damage occurred in the Air Corps. Middle ear, my father said.

Pardon me. I did not receive the gene.

The soft bones of hearing went spongy, he said—the source of distortion. "Guam," he said. The aid had whistled feedback. After a very long while or maybe a short while, a vein in the hand had been deployed to the ear, a highly adaptable channel for blood. Next came the nonstick synthetic material, surgically inserted, the same as we used to fry an egg.

"Listen," he said.

He had a finger on the oscillator. Down in the cellar, under the rooms where we slept and we read and we ate and we sat and we looked at ourselves, he used Morse Code. Ham radio. The language of pressure.

"The person to whom you are speaking," he said, "can be anywhere at all."

He asked me to practice.

"Why are you sorry now?" he said. "Couldn't you pay attention to this?"

"You can pass," my father says, "but you have to be quick. Caution causes accidents."

My father and I had had a habit together of reading in the night. We would sit on my bed on top of the covers. The book was by a physicist, written the first time in between wars, world one and two, and later revised and later translated. We took turns aloud. We shared the illustrations, the drawings of phenomena, the waves and the charts, industrious particles, ink on white. "A child can understand," he said. I think I was eight. As best I recall, we did not make it much past the opening chapter, The Air and Its Relatives.

"See?" my father said, when we came to a stop. "Now you will not need to ask, why blue."

The year it got too cold for school, my father says, he was sent on the train to an aunt in Chicago, two hours south, with nothing to do but fight with the boys with the stones along the tracks. Pipes froze. The Great Lake cracked. One day, my father says, he walked mile upon mile to that very same peninsula from which we had come, all the way out to that then-new attraction with two other boys, one of whom, my father says, would die in the war—shot out of the air, my father says—and one who could not, it turned out, afford admission. None of them entered. "Fifteen degrees below zero," he says. "You could feel the wind blowing deep in your bones."

"Shhh," my mother said.

"Baloney," he said.

She said, "People will hear you."

The time had come to pray. The place was half empty, my father in between us.

Sins were recited.

I heard him shut the prayer book and stick it in the rack. "No such thing," my father said. "There is no one in judgment."

My mother said, "What?"

Wonders and signs. Lake Forest, Waukegan, Gurnee, The City of Zion, Kenosha, Racine. North of Chicago are the towns we never enter, sights we skip. There is a lumberjack constructed out of something indestructible. Coffee and cheddar and cut-rate gas. A finger the size of a silo is pointing to gratification.

"Dad," I say.

"I am hungry," I say.

"Drive faster," he says.

"Consider the speed," my father said, regarding an occurrence in stunning replication. The panel was plastic or something translucent.

"Sound," my father said, "is slow compared to light."

I said, "Who could forget?" though I'd forgotten the gist.

People were leaving.

"Magnificent," my father said. His clothes had grown loose as a result of the treatment for corrosion of the arteries. The jacket, I saw, was ruined in an elbow. "Didn't we read about this?" he said.

"We could have," I said.

"I think so," I said.

The warning had been given.

"Refraction," he said.

He wanted to linger. Me, I can't bear to be anyplace, ever, so close to closing. I said that we must have, probably, learned this. I said we ought to go.

"Where do you think it went?" he said as I looked for an exit.

"Where do I think what went?" I said.

He said, "That book, *The Restless Universe*."

❧

Deep into summer we'd go to the lake. My father would look through a tube through a glass in the night at night. I would look at him look.

Our lake was black. Fish rose dead, silver and unseeable, and rotting by morning.

He offered the eyepiece to give me a chance. "Magnetic ropes," my father said, adjusting the view.

My mother gave a signal, a tap, a thump. It was a habit of hers. The operation had only recently succeeded; late in the night and in sleep he had been deaf, at least for practical intents.

"Inside," she said.

Light smeared the world.

"Do you see it?" he said. "Aurora borealis."

He put away the telescope and entered the tiny cottage we had rented.

Insides of rooms were the family business after the war. Recliners and sofas. Bedroom sets, dinettes, upholstered sectionals; the loveseat, the mattress, the headboard and side board, the tables for all purposes. Wood and glass, metal and varnish, quality foam. All manner of lamps with wall mounts included. Anything a body could conceivably require, with no money down, my father said.

"Lay off the horn," my father says. The throughway is torn all to pieces en route to improvement.

"Nothing is moving at all," I say.

We had seen the fish first, then walked out to view the firmament.

Exhaust fills the car.

I give it a tap, attempt a maneuver.

"No one is watching," my father says. He is licking his fingers. The bag we are eating from leaks grease.

"Touch it," he said. My father was showing me how to determine the value of a vanity. The show room was empty. "If you can poke your reflection," he said, "if there isn't any distance, you know that it's junk."

"You blinked," my father says. "It was your own hesitation."

"I'm sorry," I say.

"No matter," he says, surveying the damage. "At least it was nothing more than a taillight. Things sometimes break."

"Look for the streaks," my father said. "Now do you see?" It was chilly outside, despite being summer.

"Sure," I said.

"Do you?" he said.

Where we sat was up a hill, late at night. After a very long while, or maybe a short while, I would be older than my father was then.

"Where are you going?" my father said, and I could hear the water lapping.

CHEATERS

In the book of the night, the man and woman sleep and oversleep until the night turns to evening. They wake to the dusk. The covers are tattered, shabby. The spine is worse for wear. Whole chapters are ragged, sticky, yellowed, and fragile from touch. The woman sighs. "We are not on the same page," she says. The man does not hear, or else does not answer, as if he is someplace far from her. Significant objects fill up the bedroom: photos, keepsakes, the earrings on the dresser, the slip on the floor. These are cherished possessions indicative of character, personal quirks. "Must you?" he says. The dusk, the woman thinks, grows thicker as she rises. Outside the window the world is gone. Nevertheless, she is yanking on garments: skirt and blouse of salient label, the bracelet he gave her, clasping clasps. The man is still groggy and speaks through a yawn. "What is the conflict now?" he says. The woman turns. Space breaks between them. The phone starts to ring, and rings through a chapter. Neither one answers. He kindles the lamp. Paragraphs spill out unvoiced: Languid suspicions; an episode from childhood; a false sense of self; a shadow, if ever so faint, of hope. He watches her leaving, dressed for day. "You'll be back," he says, as if skipping ahead, as he sinks beneath covers.

FLESH, BLOOD

The woman does not want to open the door. She has failed or has neglected or refused or such—whichever you will—flat out, it can be said, to respond. The voices implore her.

The house smells of wax and of sanitary poison.

Perhaps they will believe, she tells herself, she's gone to sleep.

"Silence," said the woman. They were up in the attic— the crawlspace—again.

The neighbor had a weapon: out in the a.m., bandanna on the neck, checked vest, and fine, tanned arms. The aim too high. "Damnation," she said.

The woman—not the neighbor—was my mother, which should not surprise you. "We do not live in a place like this. Look at this. Wash," she said.

It was hanging like flags, a nation of wrung-out bodily shapes: stained, not ours, not ours—a madwoman's torso.

Ours was in the house.

What they left was evidence, a hole in the wall up

under the eave—intruders of nature—the gutter where the leaves collected in the fall.

It was supposed to be nice.

Someone would be paid for this, to settle this, or so my mother said, and winter, when it came, would do the rest.

❋

In the museum, I watched the chickens hatch. Too cold to go out—it is never as cold as it was anymore, back then: downed up and shivering. I was sent there to play, and watch the spectacle of birth.

Always there was scurrying, too many offspring, the neighbor asserted. "One is too many," I heard my mother say, although apropos of what I do not know. Quiet she liked, and weaponlessness.

You could take out an eye.

The newborns stumbled into the springtime under the glass as if stunned by the light. Their feathers were wet.

Knock on wood. I have not been in years.

The exhibit was a designated permanent fixture—but sadly, the neighborhood, my mother said, went.

❋

My mother left a message on the answering machine in which she spelled the world "nails." She asked me to call her. She asked if I were possibly already home.

It was a product she wanted—a hardening agent. "I need you to buy it and mail it," she said.

My mother's hands are lovely, I might add.

The man who was my father asked me a question: whether the house in a story I had written was symbolic of the body—but whose he did not say.

When he left, he left behind a drawer of items. We couldn't have sold them.

"What have you got in there?" the neighbor said. She was polishing a barrel.

The ceiling pouched. Birds broke and entered, carriers, wreckers of homes—then squirrels, hoarders, and last of all water.

Tap, tap, tap.

A peck on the cheek.

A rag in the voice.

The drawer was stuck, the laundry defeated, and Missus Bandanna was missing a tooth.

Still, men came to look.

"Varmints," she said.

My father left directions for the answering machine.

They are waiting out loud, as children do. There is never a minute of peace in this house, and nothing unbroken, it seems to her, not even the past, nor even her silence. Nothing is even. "Where is your father?" again and again. Not off the hook—the telephone ringing; it always is. Too many extensions. Somebody all the time listening in—cutting in— needing something, more or less.

Love me.

No moment is sacred and all of them are.

The sun is on the floor because it has to be, probably; the hand, as you'd expect, is at a knob. Already there are fingerprints.

She blinks at a threshold.

Who is the woman? Who is the woman now?

SEVEN SPELLS

1. Hungry. Crash diet. Hit the floor in the high-school corridor and get sent home. I wasn't out more than a minute, they say, insist to me. I thought that I was moving, maybe jigging uncontrollably. I still have the scar on my chin.

2. Lab class. It's called "Pests, Parasites, and Man"—an improbable freshman science class for humanities majors, kids who wouldn't stand a chance in Physics 101. It's, by the way, the only class that hadn't been closed out at registration. The lab is suffocating. Our teaching assistant, in lieu of instruction, has taken to showing us graphic film footage of infectious diseases. We've had rocky mountain fever and whatever the thing is you get from a cat that's dangerous when you're pregnant— coccidiomycosis. Today's diseases are amoebic dysentery followed by cholera. We are watching barely living skeletons expel diarrhea. There can't be any hope—by now, at the time of our viewing, they must surely be dead—yet the volunteer medics are bucketing vomit, looking with a needle for a vein. During an intubation of the neck on a patient whose veins appear to have collapsed, I fall off my lab stool and hit the concrete floor head first. I don't know where I am—or where I was—but I have been here before. Someone turns the lights on.

The teaching assistant stops the film; it sputters off. He hadn't watched it first, he concedes, before showing it to us. Perhaps, he says, this one was a bit too…he's searching for a word. Early, he says—class is let out early.

Everyone, it seems, is heading for the lakefill, our hard shore built of what has been cast off.

Back at my dorm, I look in the bathroom mirror at the gash across my forehead, the bird's egg (or is it goose?) that's starting to form. I try to do the crossword puzzle that someone has taped, along with a pencil stub on a string, to the door of a stall. My eyes hurt, so I go to my room and lie down. My roommate is elsewhere, as ever; when her parents call, as they do, I tell them she's just down the hall, in the shower, indisposed. "Dinner time," my friend says, entering while knocking. When I tell her I don't want to eat, she makes me put my shoes on to walk to the infirmary. I think this is a terrible idea.

The person who examines me says he is an "extern" and looks to me to be about my age. He shines in my eyes and listens through his stethoscope, then says he has concluded I don't have a concussion—"But," he says. But, but, but. "Do you know you have a heart murmur?" he says. He won't let me go home. When I wake up, my mother is there. "You look upset," I say. She's looking in her purse. She keeps Kleenex in her purse. Someone, she says, from the infirmary called her and told her I had a concussion. "How could you…" she says.

"Your father," she says, over club sandwiches, no middle slice. Then we go to a real doctor, who fails to find anything going on with my heart. "Concussion?" he says. "Possible." What I have are two black eyes, so we swing by the drugstore that cashes checks and stock up on concealer before my mother leaves.

The gash is scabbing over. My nose is badly swollen. People ask me whether I've been in an accident—meaning, with a car. My sweet, elderly Russian teacher tells me it's okay for me to miss the last week of class before Thanksgiving. She tells me to go home, then says something inflected that I can't understand. Walking around with pods of mismatched makeup under my eyes, I seem to make people wary. When my report card comes at the end of the term, I see that I've gotten an A in "Pests, Parasites and Man."

3. Blood test. I stand up, then fall down. The nurse can't find a pulse at first and panics. I tell her I must have one. Then I lie back down.

4. Sugar Pops—dinner—in the seventh floor walkup I share with a roommate on Thompson Street, so small that it never takes more than one ring to answer the phone (except I rarely do), before heading out with girls I know— transplanted Midwesterners, girls in search of something, or anything, too easy to impress—to a place we know in Soho. We can't afford to drink, but someone always pays for us—at least, that's what we tell ourselves. I'm wearing a delicate lavender dress that's somehow ridiculous the minute we walk in the door. It's a cavernous place, six deep to the bar. This time I sit on the floor before losing consciousness. When I come to on the sidewalk, the bouncer who carried me out wants my friends to tell him what I took. I think I've been out for hours; it feels like a hole in the night. "You'd better tell the truth," he says. Cab home—can't afford it. I never wear the dress again.

5. Eight months gone, I make a last trip home to see my mother, my father, places I grew up. Did I mention my father? He lives way down the lake. I want everything to be the way it was before I left.

The baby is kicking; perhaps he's upside down.

Leaving again, it's an hour to the airport in Milwaukee, so my father and I are up and out before the sun. He says he doesn't mind, but he's dark around the eyes. His hands are liver-spotted on the wheel. My father likes to talk about astronomy and molecules, the nature of the firmament (the infinite, he says, is in the infinitesimal), small product manufacturing (he's patented a chair designed to trigger certain brain waves), Latin music, ballroom dancing, quantum physics, aeronautics, aging. "I believe," he says, "we could extend the human life span, maybe by at least 100 years." He is eating in the car—a banana, pills. "Want some?" he says.

The plane reeks of sauce. The food cart is coming... and two women are wavering above me with an oxygen tank. They're flight attendants, uniformed. One says I had a seizure. "You made a noise," she says. The other says I need to eat right now, have this plastic tray of breakfast, which is orange juice—fine—and airline crepes in cream. I eat a few bites and start vomiting profusely. I need a second bag, a third, can't make it down the aisle to the bathroom. There's nothing but fluid. The baby isn't kicking. The man from Racine in the seat next to mine, having given me his bag, is at a loss. "I'm sorry," I say. "I'm so sorry," I say. "Air traffic"—it's the flight attendant back again, the grave one—"The captain—" What is she saying? "Could you please get ahold of yourself?" she says.

Forty minutes early, we're at LaGuardia, as if there were a secret route through distance and time. Some people seem annoyed by time to kill. The paramedics take me off, cuff my arm. My blood pressure alarms them. "Look at this," says one to the other. "Will you look?" There are two of everyone today, it seems. They want to take me to Jamaica hospital; I insist on going to a pay phone (my dime). The paramedics make me sign a waiver stating that I'm knowingly ignoring their advice.

By the time I get to my doctor, 20 minutes later, the baby is active. We listen to the heartbeat. "You're fine," my doctor says. "Go home and eat starch." I call my husband, who goes out to buy crackers.

When I call my dad, I say my flight arrived the better part of an hour early. "Really," he says. "That never happens to me."

6. Labor room. Everyone is leaving. The nurse slips out; my doctor, who is pregnant (what a sight we must be!) takes a swollen ankle break, and my husband—we've done this before—is buying something for a headache. My father's parents, who are dead, come into the room together. Everything is fine with them. The baby is fine, fine, fine. I am very happy. A woman is screaming. Something is slapped on my face and I open my eyes and I'm under an oxygen mask. "Delivery!" the woman says. My husband's face appears. I'm lifted, heaved and wheeled. "Is there oxygen in there?" my doctor keeps asking. My grandparents—people are yelling at me. "Push! Push-push!" There's a whole crowd in here. Someone checks the plastic mask I'm pushing off my face. I feel the baby leaving me. They take away the baby. Then they bring the baby back, and then he looks at me and takes my breast, and then they take him away again.

I am on the phone, leaving messages for everyone. No one is home. Later a doctor enters my room and tells me not to worry; he's checked the baby over and the baby is fine. "Why wouldn't he be?" I ask. The doctor wants to know if I remember him—the whole team, with the crash cart. I shake my head no.

7. Tetanus shot—preventative; why wait for a rusty nail? ("Do you know what lockjaw looks like?" my mother used to say.) I pay my co-pay and collapse. Women in the waiting

room are swooning over me. It was quicker than I think, they say, of shorter duration, this blackout or spell. I thought that I was home, in a room that is gone, and also somehow in motion. The receptionist is speaking with a certain irritation. "Your patient—" she says to the intercom system. She makes me eat a cracker, two crackers from somewhere, left over from lunch. "I don't like this," my doctor says, reading a meter. She won't let me look. When she lets me stand, I can't make it to the door.

The doctor calls at night. She wants to talk to me; she is talking to me about things that end in "noma." I fire her.

I get worked up. Knock on wood. No noma, the endocrinologist says. He has a name for my condition, which I make him repeat. It escapes me again.

The babies have birthdays. My grandfather appears in a dream where he's carrying the body of a man I can't identify. My father sits down swiftly, surprisingly gracefully, witnesses say, while dancing, and never gets back up. When I call the house, I get his voice on the machine but the body is elsewhere, in storage, is ash.

There are no more spells. I am learning things, like when to keep my head down and the uses of salt.

NO PLACE ON EARTH

"Which would you rather be?" she says. "A rock or an insect?"

"Rock," he says. He is pressing his face to the glass again.

"Why?" she says.

"Rock crushes insect."

"What if the insect's huge?" she says.

The boy turns. The bus stops. "Huge," he says. He pushes his face against her chest. "Until it meets the rock."

"Not our stop," she says.

Winter is on them, ice on the trees. Roads have been salted.

The boy's pale skin is damp from the window. His skin is like hers.

"I know that," he says, and sits back down.

His breath on the glass is the matter through which she views the world. It is late afternoon; the heat too high, the sky about to darken.

Her ankles are swollen, belly, her breasts.

"Smarty," she says. She loosens his scarf. She crawls her fingers up his neck. So soft, the boy! "Then where did you think you were going, you?"

❉

"A sister or brother?"

"Silly," she'd said. "You will be a brother."

❉

A snapshot she keeps on the mantel at home. Look at her: the size the boy is now. Afraid of her shadow. Clearly it is afternoon, the light in a slant.

She was posed on a boulder for added height.

The stone is not visible.

"Reason you're tall," her brother had said, "is that I am holding you up."

❉

"Here is a brand new fact," she says. "Salt erodes rock."

The boy asks a question she cannot answer.

"Water," she says.

What was she thinking? Wrong for a child—the scarf he wears. A purchase on impulse, too hand-made, an afterthought, or no thought at all. Rummage. Who knew where things came from? The tassels are wet.

"Jupiter or Mars?" he says. "Where would you rather—"

"Rather be"—an end, not an answer.

A window or fist? A wish or a feather? Candy or rain. "Rain," he says. "Don't want to be eaten."

❈

"Look at it, look out the window," she says. Ice falls in drops. She smells the boy's neck from the back, the nape; his smell a narcotic, impermanent, impossible—she knows it, she does. You do not have to tell her. Bottle it up.

"Rain," he says.

"Then I will drink you."

❈

Someone is listening in on them. She hears the woman listen, behind her, intent.

❈

He is sipping a drink from a box she brought. Provisions on her person, always, she thinks. Things stuck to her—a pouch, a container, fluid. Retention.

She says, "I see the future."

His hair appears slick, poking out from a cap. He is sleepy, she thinks. Must be sleepy, she thinks. You are getting sleepy.

A wish if there was one.

Nausea, or craving, is creeping over her.

"Ask me?" he asks her. "Ask me again."

❈

Outside the window, seen through a smear: a school she once went to, a world subsumed—there's nothing as it used to be. "Winter was colder then," she says.

"When?" he says.

She turns to look behind her.

❋

The boy makes legs on her arms with his fingers.

"Listen," she says. "I would walk home alone, unless my brother was along." The day that she stripped off her mittens, she says, her brother was someplace, no place, gone. "I wanted to touch the snow with my fingers. Snowballs and angels." She touches his hand. "Please, don't do that."

"Which would you rather be?" he says. "A snowball or angel?"

"I mean it," she says. "I was crying from cold when he found me there."

"Who?" he says.

"Frostbite."

She sees the boy regarding her. Blue, his eyes. She will not tell the boy what she did not tell her brother, her father. What is her job if not to protect? Protect the protectors! "Hands," she says. "An officer returned me home. My mother ran water."

❋

The boy is still watching. His mittens are sensibly clipped to his sleeves; they dangle there. He chews the scarf's tassels, caught in the act.

"Foolish," she says. She feels the chill seeping, the gray

of the sky. The driver has killed the heat, she thinks. Hands—
the car, the gray of the light.

The parts of her frozen.

Salt destroys rock.

"Angel licks snowball." The boy is a boy.

"Always wear your gloves," she says.

❋

Hours at the reservoir, fields, the road, looking for this
or that to fear, and finding it, mostly. The boy will not travel
alone, she thinks, at least not till he's older and older again.
The girl is the mother of the child.

She is kicked from within.

The doors open and close.

❋

It is all of it used—a saturated wrapper, a patch from a
snowsuit, a scarf, too large, in a favorite color.

Hood, sleeve, hat, boot.

A hole from somebody else's exertions.

See the boy lean into her! "When?" he says. "Mama?
When will we be there?"

"Mars?" she says.

"Don't," he says.

"Soon," she says. "Sooner or later."

❋

Later her husband will carry the boy, beloved and
sleeping, aloft, to bed.

Later she'll take the hat, the kiss, the wet scarf unraveling.
Later she will say to him, "A bushel or a peck?"

❋

All of the houses are yellow-lit, diffuse through the
windows. Her belly is growing, even as she rides.
Later the children, as children do, will shield her the
best that they can from her lapses, at least for a while.
"A wish or a feather?" the boy demands.
"Wish," she says.
He says, "A feather is real."

❋

Later she'll think there was nobody listening in at all.
That woman has vanished.

❋

"Look," she says. The street is theirs. The doors have
been opened.
He rubs his eyes.
She's got his hand.
"Home," she says.
The boy appears stunned, as if freshly awake. "Where?"
he says. "Where would you rather be?"

BEYOND ALL BLESSING AND SONG, PRAISE AND CONSOLATION

Mother is singing. It is afternoon again, or it is night, maybe later, an end of a day we have lived in our house, we have spent in our house; we are restless and lying in the glittering dark.

She is singing of Kentucky.

Mother, so far as we know her, has never much left the Midwest. La, la, go the words when she cannot remember.

The sheets smell of yard. The yard smells of burning: Grill, brickette.

Meat.

Leaves.

We will sing for our supper: Listen to us!

There's a trellis out front of roses that climb and that won't always be here, Mother has said. "Will not, do you hear me?" Mother has said, and not to us, and we have heard.

Mother's hair is thick and dark. The voice is still darker. The wrist has a scent. It is some type of flower or essence—reduction—or mineral or element.

Carbon.

You is mighty lucky, Babe of old Kentucky.

Wisconsin is our residence, second generation; lucky to be here and eager to leave. Mother is first.

Men appear to like to look. And why would they not? Our mother is a beauty.

Our mother—and don't you forget it—is ours.

We will sing of the places we will not go.

We will dress in her clothes: grosgrains, velveteens, moirés, swiss-dot samples, sequined bits. The belts and the darts! The height of our mother in shoes dyed to match! Silk if for night. See her drawing a blind.

Our father has left or is leaving again.

He is up in the air. He is standing on a wing in an aviator jacket.

Hand on hat.

Rose on wood.

Oil and water: Mother paints. All over the house are the scenes she has hung.

Her feet are in slippers, her voice in our sleep.

Skin, lamb.

We are counting our blessings, as Grandfather says. The food on the table: sugared and boiled, buttered, cured. Silver and tallow. The jelly is mint. "Vot is this?"—he says to us, the accent congealed.

We are lifting a glass.

Our father is back, if not for long. Our father will fly us away with him, my sister and I. There is always an attraction. Statues, valleys, cities we have heard of, and one we have not. Glasgow, Kentucky: Mammoth Cave. The smell is of sulfur. Kill the lantern. Feel your death. The guide strikes a match for us, a glow in the dark. There is a crowd in the earth. These are sensible people, and also us.

A national treasure, our grandfather says.

Nights we eat biscuits, syrup on something, a souvenir spot.

Mother is calling and calling again. We are waiting for parts. Our plane has been grounded. Oil is spilt. The medium has changed, she says, and now it is ink.

Rock, paper, scissors.

Tears.

Milk.

Waking again, it is winter again, it is autumn again—but never, the way it is sung of, spring—and sooty at a window. We will not budge. Mother is not getting younger, she says. Her cough is fresh. There is a rancor in the kitchen, a sash uncinched. "Here," she says. "There," she says. "Eat," she says. "La, la."

Men have come to move the earth. Boots, hands. The size of them! Unsupervised and dangerous: Here's what the job is, Mother will say. A handle is busted, a stone unturned.

My sister and I have unburied a hatchet. Who loves who the most of all?

"Whom," says our mother.

The postcards are albumed, smeary with want, the range needs attention, and, wouldn't you know, we have incinerated something. Tourist trap: We knew as much. A sore point of interest. The mail comes and goes. My sister and I are collecting a collection of itinerate postmarks.

Warned, we lick.

Mother has rendered a likeness of us, an indelible expression, double or nothing. Crinoline. Patent. Heels. A purse. Accessories of Mother, in darkened silhouette.

There's a coin in a pocket—rainy day; a medal our father has saved from the Air Corps. Copper or ribbon: We'd know what it is if we found it again.

Fly away! Poor wet wren; the birdbath is flooded, my sister says. Equipment is failing. The charcoal is almost entirely wrecked.

Mother is singing in spite of words. "What am I to do," she says, "with everyone leaving." Crank up jalopy: Here is her father, a bud in the hat. The heart is nipped, tucked up a sleeve. Old refugee. "I am the viper," the punchline goes. "Vould you like your vindows vashed?" Hysteria, always. But vot is the joke? We are nailed to the wall. The frame is on us.

It is damp in the earth as a matter of course. A traveler ought to have practical footwear.

"Never," says Mother, or maybe "now," atotter with glamor, going off.

There is a monument to something—a place we might have photographed.

Give us your tired, deliberating souls.

The people in town, such as it is, sit on the curb and watch the road go nowhere.

Our feet stick and blister. The farmer's in the dell again. The mind cannot stay. We are wandering off, or over and out, paired and turned sideways. Time and again, we cannot tell the difference: Which are stalactites, anyway?

Mother is humming, a man on her arm. It is summer again, and it is time to prune the roses, pin the gardenias, trim the clinquant snippets. Season the grill.

Salt, pepper, incense.

Wing and a prayer.

We cannot sleep. There is nobody home. Except for us. Mother has posed and redressed us again: an age she was—or some of the ages Mother has been. We are as she has made us, more and less.

Features, not substance.

Bones.

Paste.

Mother says, "Look." She says, "Look at the light."

We are looking at feet.

An aisle is swaying. Rugs ruck up. Again, again, she sings off-pitch, our mother does: a crack in the alto, strings unstrung. It is the hand that is unholdable. Mother drops a syllable, an octave, bags, a delicate matter; breaks a sweat. She disidentifies us. It is dollars to donuts. Dust to dust. The fathers are buried: hers, ours. Bread and roast and cake again, release and reunion—who wants more? We lick our plates.

Mother, untethered, will travel, she says, pretty please: La, la. The gifts she will bring us—wrapped, undone. An empire waits.

A vessel has burst.

We cannot look. We cannot but look.

Men are in the yard again. The body of Mother. A foregone conclusion, Mother would say. The heart is a pump. In the end, it quits.

I will speak for myself: There is no end.

I am calling and calling.

The candles are lit.

ACKNOWLEDGMENTS

These acknowledgments could go on longer than my stories, but in particular, I would like to express my gratitude to Melanie Jackson, to the Dzanc crew—Dan Wickett (arguably the hardest working man in indie publishing), Steve Gillis, Mary Gillis and Steven Seighman, to Marc Chenetier, Monica Manolescu-Oancea and the Observatoire de Litterature Amercaine at the University of Paris for encouragement and incitement when it was much needed, to Gordon Lish, to Terese Svoboda and to Diane Williams. Finally and always, to Mike Evers and our sons, Brendan and Sean. Hey, Sean—thanks for the cover drawing.